GW00992234

Daniel Hargreaves

I Wish I Could

A Make-Believe Story

I Wish I Could

By Dean Walley

Illustrated by Arlene Noel

♕ HALLMARK CHILDREN'S EDITIONS

I Wish I Could

I wish I could fly. Then I'd look inside clouds and climb over the rainbow to see what's really at the end. When I saw a bird going somewhere, I could go along too.

Sometimes I'd fly very fast. Faster than the wind. And sometimes I'd fly very slowly over my town and watch all the people below. When I came to my house, I'd just drift in one spot in the air and wave at everyone.

That's the way it would be if I could fly.

I wish I could be big. Really big. As big as a house and as tall as a tree. When I'd walk, it would make a sound like "Boom Boom Boom" and the ground would shake. Everybody would look at me and say, "Look at him! Have you ever seen anyone so big?" And I'd smile at them, so they wouldn't be afraid.

If I got tired of being big, I'd want to be
little. Not just little like a baby. Really little.
So little I could sit on a penny and have lots of
room left over. So little I could take a ride
on an ant and see where he lives.

It would be fun to go for a swim in a dewdrop. I could take a nap on a blade of grass and go all kinds of places where regular people can't go— like inside a soap bubble. That's how I'd take my bath.

I wish I could be two people instead of just one. Both of me would look just like me. Then one of me could do all the things I'm supposed to do. And the other of me could do whatever I want.

At night, while one of me sleeps, the other of me would be out having lots of adventures. Then the next morning the tired me could stay in bed while the me that had rested goes to school.

If I could be two people I could eat twice as much candy. I could even play checkers with myself. Sometimes both of me would go to parties together and surprise everyone.

I wish I could change into all kinds of different animals. Then if I wanted to, I could be a dog and see how it feels to wag my tail and bark. It would be fun to be a giraffe, unless I had a sore throat.

If I were a lion, I'd surprise
everyone by being very friendly
and only growling once in a while.

Every day I'd change myself into
something different, but at night I'd
come back home and be me. Mother
wouldn't like it if an elephant slept
in my bed.

I wish I could do magic things. Then
if it were time to carry out the trash,
I could just say some magic words like,
"Ooom Piffle Waffle Poof" and
the trash would disappear.

I would have a magic wand so I
could change people into frogs.
But just for a little while.

And my magic ring would help me
make all kinds of things appear like
bikes and puppies and lollipops.

I might even have a magic hat to
make me extra smart. I could wear
it to school.

I wish I could be invisible. Then nobody would know when I was around. I could play tricks on people and find out secrets.

Of course, I'd have some invisible clothes. In the winter I'd have an invisible coat and invisible galoshes. Everybody would say, "Who's building that snowman?"

I wish I could have a secret place. It would
be in the middle of a big forest. I would
have my own secret river and my
own secret valley.

I'd build a secret house and inside it
would be a secret box where I'd keep all
kinds of secret things.

Once in a while, I'd take somebody
there. But only special people. I'd blindfold
them and twirl them around a lot so they'd
never remember how to get there.

I wish I could make all my wishes come true. Don't you?